D1224232

Copyright © 2003 by Sally Grindley
Illustrations copyright © 2003 by Michael Terry

All rights reserved.
No part of this book may be used or reproduced
in any manner whatsoever without written permission from
the publisher except in the case of brief quotations
embodied in critical articles or reviews.

Published by Bloomsbury, New York and London
Distributed to the trade by St. Martin's Press

Library of Congress Cataloging-in-Publication Data:
Grindley, Sally.
The sulky vulture/Sally Grindley and Michael Terry (illustrator). p.cm.
Summary: Boris the vulture sulks because he doesn't like the food his parents eat or the games his
friends play, and even a cuddle from his mother gives him reason to fuss.
ISBN 1-58234-794-8 (alk. paper)
[1. Vultures--Fiction. 2. Behavior--Fiction.] I. Terry, Michael, ill. II. Title.
PZ7.G88446 Su 2003
[E]--dc21
2002019114

First U.S. Edition 2003
Printed in Belgium by Proost

1 3 5 7 9 10 8 6 4 2

Bloomsbury USA Children's Books
175 Fifth Avenue
New York, New York 10010

The Sulky Vulture

by Sally Grindley

illustrations by Michael Terry

BLOOMSBURY
CHILDREN'S
BOOKS

DERRY PUBLIC LIBRARY
64 E. BROADWAY
DERRY, NH 03038

"Eat your dinner," said Boris's mother.

"Don't like meat," said Boris.

"Then go without," said Boris's dad.

Off stomped Boris with a "Humph."

Head pulled down, shoulders hunched up, toes curled in,
Boris the vulture was sulking.

"What's the matter, Boris?" said Leo the leopard.

"I don't like meat," said Boris.

"Never mind, Boris," said Leo.

"Let's play a game of tag."

Leo chased Boris and caught him right away.
Boris chased Leo ... but Leo was too fast.

"I've had enough of this," grumbled Boris.

Head pulled down, shoulders hunched up, toes curled in,
Boris the vulture was sulking.

"What's the matter, Boris?" said Flora the zebra.

"I don't like playing tag," said Boris.

"Never mind, Boris," said Flora,
"Let's play hide-and-seek."

Boris hid behind a tree ... Flora found him
right away. Flora hid in some grass ...

Boris couldn't find her though he looked and looked and looked.

"I've had enough of this," he grumbled.

Derry Public Library

Head pulled down, shoulders hunched up, toes curled in,
Boris the vulture was sulking.

"What's the matter, Boris?" said Tara the elephant.
"I don't like hide-and-seek," said Boris.

"Never mind, Boris," said Tara,
"Let's throw coconuts."

"Bet I can throw the farthest," said Boris.

Boris threw a coconut …

Tara threw one farther.

Boris threw another,

and hit a rhino on the head.

The rhino charged …
Boris leapt up into a tree,

and the rhino just
missed him!

Head pulled down, shoulders hunched up, toes curled in,
Boris the vulture was sulking.

"What's the matter, Boris?" asked Marvin the baboon.
"I don't like rhinos," said Boris.

"Never mind, Boris," said Marvin,
"Come and swing."

Boris climbed on ...
Marvin gave him a push.

Forwards Boris went,
and backwards again.

Forwards he went,
and backwards again.

Higher he went.
And higher.
And higher.

"This is fun!" he cried.

'Harder, push me harder!'

Marvin pushed him harder and …

… the swing broke.

Head pulled down, shoulders hunched up, toes curled in,
Boris the vulture was sulking.

"What's the matter, Boris?" said Boris's mother.

"I don't like meat, and I don't like playing tag.
I don't like hide-and-seek and I don't like throwing
coconuts. I don't like swings and — can I have a
cuddle?"

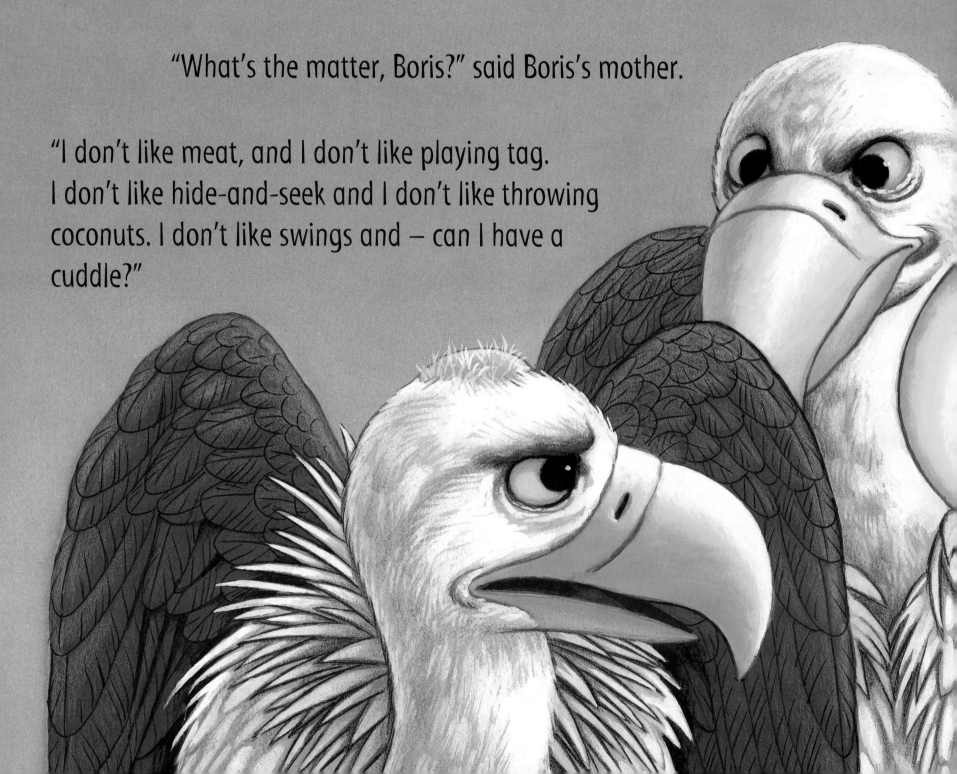

"Of course you can," said Boris's mother.
"I'll give you a great big cuddle ...
and then it's time for bed."

"But I don't like bed!" shouted Boris.